For Nic

Big thank-you to Mum, Dad, Jade, Luisa, Mike, Anita,
and Kelly — who all helped me get Nowhere

First edition 2013

Library of Congress Catalog Card Number 2012947828
ISBN 978-0-7636-6367-4

13 14 15 16 17 18 TLF 10 9 8 7 6 5 4 3

Printed in Dongguan, Guangdong, China

This book was typeset in Carrotflower.
The illustrations were done in mixed media, including cardboard.

Candlewick Press
99 Dover Street
Somerville, Massachusetts 02144

visit us at www.candlewick.com

CANDLEWICK PRESS

THE NOWHERE BOX

SAM ZUPPARDI

George's little brother was being
a real nuisance.

So was his even
littler brother.

Everywhere George went

the littler boys
followed.

George had had enough!

The box from the
washing machine
was just what
George needed.

In no time, he was ready for his escape.

George pressed a button . . .

and
he
was
Nowhere.

Nowhere was vast and empty . . .

but not for long.

Soon Nowhere was amazing!

Nowhere was magnificent!

Nowhere was stupendous!

Meanwhile, George's little brothers were wondering where he'd gone.

He wasn't in the bedroom.

He wasn't in the bathroom.

He wasn't in the living room.

Where was George?

He was Nowhere.

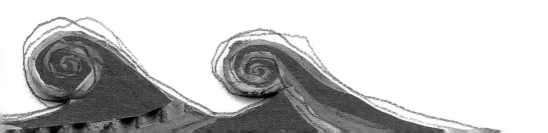

But in Nowhere there were no enemy pirates in sight.

And there were no dragons to be found.

In fact, there was no one at all.

And that's when George realized...

he knew just where to find great
enemy pirates . . . and pretty good
dragons, too.

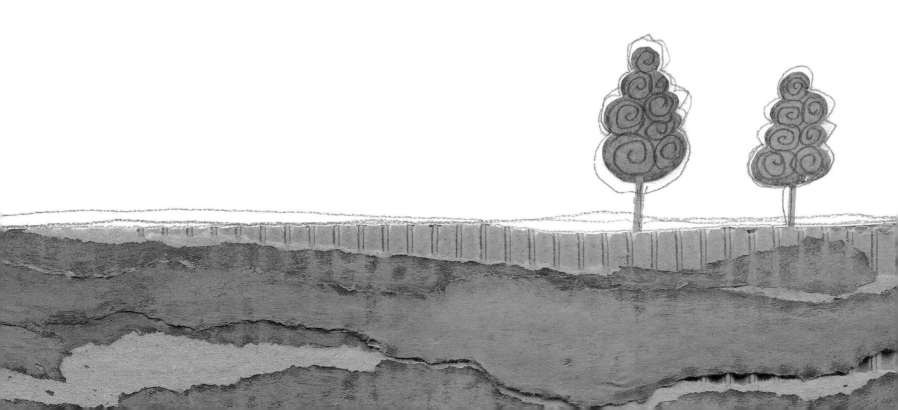

With that thought, he hopped
back in his ship...

and set a course for home.